GHOSTLY ENCOUNTERS OF GETTYSBURG

As told by:

Johlene "Spooky" Riley

To Andrew
Great meeting you!
Johlene Spooky

D1444410

Edited by:
Hannah Wicklein

FIRST EDITION

Printed and bound in the United States of America

Printed by: SEABER TURNER ASSOCIATES
436 Coronet Drive
Blandon, PA 19510

Published by: ARBOR HOUSE AT GETTYSBURG INC.
47 Steinwehr Avenue
Gettysburg, PA 17325
717-338-1818

ISBN-978-0-9835573-0-2

Cover Design by: Greg Briggs, Sarah Hoffman, Johlene "Spooky" Riley and Hannah Wicklein
Celtic Scroll Design by: Greg Briggs

To my son, Patrick, who has never stopped believing in me. He will always be the most important thing that I have ever created.

The boundaries which divide Life from Death are at best shadowy and vague. Who shall say where the one ends, and where the other begins?

-Edgar Allen Poe

Table of Contents

Acknowledgements

So many individuals were instrumental in making this book possible. Without their contributions these stories would remain untold. I wish to acknowledge the following people.

My parents, Patrick and Ruth Riley, who instilled the love of storytelling and good work ethics in me at a young age. The loving home they provided for me and the encouragement they gave so freely has never been forgotten. Although they are no longer with us here on earth, they will always be in my heart and with me every step of the way. My son, Patrick, who has been an inspiration to me from the very day he was born. His loyalty, intellect and generosity have never ceased to amaze me. He has been my rock of Gibraltar when things were almost too difficult to bear. He is truly my gift from God. Peter Riley, my younger brother, who watched all of those scary ghost movies with me as a child and who helps to keep me from taking myself too seriously.

The talented staff of Gettysburg Ghost Tours and Gettysburg Paranormal Association, whose teamwork and skills have been invaluable to me.

I wish to thank Susan Saum-Wicklein and George Lomas for allowing me the freedom to pursue my dreams and an avenue in which to facilitate them as well as their kindness and friendship. Hannah Wicklein, my editor, who spent many hours and much patience with me to make this, my first book, a book worthy of reading.

Chris Taylor, one of the most talented storytellers I have had the pleasure of knowing, whose friendship, encouragement and laughter have been an incredible inspiration to me during this endeavor.

Thank you to the many people who have crossed my path and have been generous enough to share their experiences with me for this book. Last, but certainly not least, I want to share my appreciation to the scores of "Spooky" fans that have been anxiously awaiting this book. They have been loyal, enthusiastic and have stayed up late into the night with me looking for the restless spirits of Gettysburg.

Introduction

I saw my very first ghost when I was about three years old. I remember insisting that one of my parents stay with me in my bedroom until I safely fell asleep. Most nights I would see a large dog sitting on the floor next to my bed. My parents, particularly my father, would try to convince me that it was only my imagination. I just knew that they were wrong. I saw that dog right up until my bedroom was moved to the second floor of the house.

Throughout my childhood, I would have déjà vu moments and times where I could tell people what they were about to say before they uttered a word. I really never gave it much thought, though. I enjoyed the typical childhood. Most days were spent outdoors, playing with friends or my brothers. It was a happy childhood with many great memories. Both of my parents were wonderful storytellers and would delight my younger brother and I by telling us elaborate tales before bedtime. It's no wonder I ended up being a professional storyteller myself. One might say it was in my blood.

One story that truly captivated me was the story of Black Aggie. She was a statue in the nearby cemetery that was a local legend. Supposedly, she was haunted by a curse and anyone who looked into her black marble eyes or spent the night in her outstretched arms were doomed. I had a fascination with things that could not be explained away. It wasn't until I was fifteen that I saw another spirit. This time, it was an apparition of a woman wearing a long gray dress. She would whip quickly around the corner and into the kitchen. This time, I wasn't the only one who saw her. My father saw her in the kitchen as well. She even brushed past him as she went by.

I was hooked at this point. I had a real need for answers. Why do ghost exists and how? This curiosity, coupled with my ability to connect with these spirits, led me down the paranormal path I have taken. I hope that in some way, this collection of true stories will inspire my readers to search for answers as well.

Old Number One

1861

Phoenix Iron Company. Phoenixville, Pennsylvania

"Stamp it," a voice says gruffly. The three-inch artillery tube is the first to be accepted by the government.

A young man, barely more than a boy, brushes his cloth against the dark metal of the tube, cleaning away the last bits of grease and dust.

* * *

I gazed out my window, and couldn't help but smile. It would be my first evening as a tour guide for a popular ghost tour company in Gettysburg. There was a momentary flutter in my stomach but I pushed it aside as I turned my attention back to the closet, pondering what outfit would work best.

I pushed hanger after hanger aside, studying each piece of clothing, and then moved on. Nothing seemed to speak to me but I knew one dress, one shirt, one skirt, one special something would reach out and pull me to it, just like this new job had.

My hand paused over a pitch black Victorian dress. It would be perfect. As I slipped it on, I slowly transformed into character. I fit the part I was to portray. After guiding the lace gloves over my hands, I added the final touch - a black veil. Passing the oval mirror in my parlor I stopped, momentarily staring at the mysterious woman in black before me. It was no longer a costume. I lowered the long veil over my features and the present day disappeared.

* * *

1863

"Reload," shouts a voice. It has been a long two years for Number One, its wheels rolling over what would become landmarks in history – Second Bull Run, Antietam, South Mountain, Fredericksburg, Chancellorsville, As a part of the First Corp, it travels nonstop from one fight to the next.

The wheels have cracked and needed repairs multiple times. The once gleaming barrel is scratched and will never gleam again from the blood that has been spilt all around it, and because of it.

* * *

The sun was just setting as I emerge from the Civil War Era home I was renting. I breathed in the crisp air and smiled. It was beginning. The streets appeared busy. I was confident it would be a good night for tours. As people walked past me along the narrow sidewalks, I almost felt invisible, like a ghost under the black veil of the "Widow."

My stride quickened as I saw the black cat sign and the crowds of people milling on the streets. This was the moment.

* * *

July 1ˢᵗ, 1863

West of Gettysburg, Pennsylvania.

"Keep moving forward." There is no room for discussion in the middle of the crossfire Reynold's Battery has found themselves in. The Confederate artillery continues its assault on the Union, offering no reprieve from the deadly fire.

There are shouts as Captain John A. Reynolds lets out a weak cry, clasping a hand to his eye. Blood seeps through his fingers and several men are forced to pull the Captain back, leaving Lieutenant George Breck in command. The situation is desperate, and growing worse by the second.

The constant barrage of cannon and rifle fire leaves the Battery exposed. Reinforcements cannot keep up with the death toll.

With a growl of frustration, Lieutenant Breck is forced to order the retreat along the Chambersburg Pike. Slowly, the troops withdraw, followed by the artillery, but the Pike finds itself bogged down by the retreating foot soldiers, and the cannons' retreat slows.

Even as the soldiers assigned to the protection of Number One urge their horses faster, they fall in a storm of lead, ripping through both man and animal.

With no defenders to ward off the Confederate forces, Number One is captured.

* * *

There was no tremor in my hands as I pushed open the screen door to the small shop. The bell atop the door quivered and alerted the staff that I had arrived. Everyone was all smiles and I was introduced to those I had not already met.

"Full tour tonight," I was told and I turned to accept my lantern and a few quick words of encouragement from those who would hold down the fort while I was gone.

Darkness fell at last and it was time for the journey to begin. A journey I would be making for many nights to come, but this was to be the first. It's funny how you seem to always remember your firsts. I swung the screen door open and greeted my guests. As they cast their gaze upon me, I could sense their anticipation. I would not disappoint them.

I led my group behind the shop where an old cannon sat in the quaint backyard, nestled into a corner, grass and flowers growing around its wheels.

"Good evening. I will be your tour guide... my name is Spooky, and I've earned every single letter of it, for I attract the ghosts."

I waited a moment to allow people to react, and then looked to the retired cannon.

"This is a special cannon," I began, resting one gloved hand on the barrel. "If you look closely at the muzzle, you'll see some markings that were put there in 1861, marking it as the first three inch barrel to be accepted by our government."

A guest leaned toward the barrel of the gun but quickly scrunched up his nose.

"What's wrong?" his girlfriend questioned.

The gentleman said he could smell gunpowder.

"While Number One is still in firing condition, it hasn't been fired in decades." I paused and gave a mischievous look. "Perhaps it's haunted."

The crowd laughed and I finished my introduction and led them off on their tour around Gettysburg, but my mind remained on Number One.

Pictures are frequently taken around the old cannon during tours and several images are speckled with glowing orbs. There are no explanations for these orbs, and they appear at random. Occasionally, the resulting photo shows a full-bodied apparition of a Union Soldier standing beside the cannon.

There are no identifications to name this long departed soldier, no explanation for why, so many years after the end of the War, he still guards the cannon.

Maybe he is awaiting the return of a brother-in-arms, or perhaps he refuses to leave Number One unguarded, letting such an important piece of our history fall into enemy hands once more.

Ectoplasm surrounding Number One
Photo courtesy of Anonymous

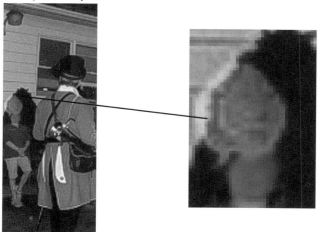

Ghostly Face by little girl next to Number One
Photo courtesy of Johlene "Spooky" Riley

Forever They May Roam

It was January first, New Year's Day. As usual, I was out and about in search of ghosts. I decided to explore "Iverson's Pitts" as this particular field is often referred to. It has been a popular destination among ghost hunters of all ages. The weather that day was typical for our region that time of year, cold and windy. Armed with a camera and a thermos of hot coffee I was on my way.

My first thought was, "Why on earth did I choose such a frigid cold day like today for this adventure?" However, I soon forgot about the chill in the air as I made my way to the tree line just ahead of me. Peering into the woods I felt as if I were not alone.

I have been a sensitive as far back as I remember. It's a strange feeling and hard to explain. Many times I have been able to detect a spirit's presence before it's been captured on film or felt by others. For some unknown reason they are drawn to me. Perhaps they can tell that I have great empathy for them. Most of the time I am truly grateful for this gift I have been given, but it is a different story altogether when I experience an emotional response that is deeply negative. I can, at times, see entire scenes right before my eyes. Can you imagine how difficult it is to watch a regiment of war-weary men charging into the jaws of certain death? I knew the soldiers were so very close. I could feel it.

Looking over my shoulder, I could still see the Doubleday Inn, a B&B sitting on the battlefield. I took comfort in knowing civilization was not very far from where I stood. Taking a deep breath, I managed enough courage to walk several yards into the woods. I admit my knees were trembling just a bit and not necessarily because of the cold. All six of my senses were on high alert. I was keenly aware of where this path was leading me.

The hallowed ground I walked on was named after Alfred Iverson Jr., a Confederate general who served during the Civil War. Much to his chagrin, Iverson was best known for his ill-fated decision on the first day of battle, which sent many men to their death. On July 1st, 1863, four North Carolina regiments were sent far too hastily into battle. Iverson failed to send scouts ahead for reconnaissance, which his men paid for. They were caught in a deadly ambush of Union troops hiding behind the stone walls to the North East of town, along what is now called Doubleday Avenue. All but a handful of the Tar Heels were slaughtered: in fact, his brigade suffered 458 casualties within seconds, falling neatly into rows where they were shot. When the helpless soldiers who somehow survived the brutal attack raised their white handkerchiefs to halt further Union fire, he called them cowards. This from a man who failed to accompany his men into battle. General Iverson later found over 600 of his men dead and wounded in what he described as "a line straight out of a dress parade." Iverson was removed from command for the remainder of the battle as his conduct had become irrational and speculation was that he was a drunkard.

Burials were swift. Mass shallow graves were dug along the very trenches where the soldiers had fallen victim to the volley of lead. It wasn't until seven years later that the Southern families of those men had finally managed to save up enough money to have their boys exhumed and returned home to Southern soil. Unfortunately, over those seven long years, most had forgotten just exactly where those bodies were located. Some of the Rebels were left on what they would have considered the wrong side of the Mason-Dixon Line for all of eternity.

I stood very still, trying to connect with those soldiers who marched bravely into battle that sweltering July day. As I stood in silence, I could hear the gusts of wind and the barren tree branches swaying back and forth, as they rattled and fell to the ground. After what must have been over half an hour, I thought that perhaps I was mistaken and I would not experience any paranormal activity that day. I poured myself a cup of coffee, hoping to warm up a bit before heading back to my car.

As I raised the plastic mug to my lips, I heard a cry that sent chills down my spine. I shall never forget it as long as I live. It sounded male and in terrible pain. It was followed by several additional cries and thuds. Was I hearing the agonizing, last desperate screams of those Southern soldiers, as they were falling one by one to their death? Were these restless spirits left here on this field to relive their horror over and over again?

I shouted as loud as I could, "Where are you?"

There was no response.

I was finally rewarded for my patience. I had been right. I was not alone. I spotted a soldier looking at me from behind a tree not more than ten feet in front of me. I remember the solemn expression he wore so vividly, even to this day. His face was careworn by the elements, prematurely aged and mostly hidden behind a beard and moustache. A pipe dangled from his lips. Atop his head he wore a cap of some sort, which was torn, and tattered. I hadn't felt as if I were in danger and I somewhat foolishly took a step in his direction and he vanished out of sight. Gone without a trace. I waited several more minutes, hoping he would reappear.

When he didn't, I prepared to head back to my car as the temperature was dropping and nightfall would soon arrive. When I reached the Doubleday Inn, I took out my camera and took a few shots in the direction of those woods I had entered. At first glance it looked like I may have captured an orb in the one frame. Not terribly impressed, I turned my camera off, hopped in my car and left. It wasn't until several weeks later that I discovered that the "orb" was actually the head of the soldier I had encountered on the battlefield that first day of January, his face forever frozen in his expression of sadness.

Area around Doubleday Avenue
Photo courtesy of Hannah Wicklein

Orb by Doubleday Avenue
Photo courtesy of Johlene "Spooky" Riley

Close up of the Orb by Doubleday Avenue

Help Us If You Can

I recall my first visit to the Haunted Creek Bed. I was following the route on a walking tour in order to familiarize myself with the stops I would soon be visiting myself. Another woman, Alice, was shadowing as well. We gathered around the guide to hear her presentation. She hadn't even begun to speak when suddenly Alice and I turned to one another.

"Did you hear that?" Alice whispered to me.

"Yes!" I replied.

We had both heard "Help me," coming from the dark water below us. I knew that I had to return here to investigate this phenomenon. Alice, on the other hand, never returned for the job as a tour guide.

Later that same week, I went back to the creek to see what I could discover. I brought my usual assortment of paranormal equipment with me to document and to verify any experiences I might have. Even though I am a sensitive, it was important to provide scientific data to support my findings. My first task was to take a temperature reading. Initially, the devise registered 39 degrees, only to drop to a bone chilling 10 degrees within seconds. There was the distinct possibility that there was a spirit using the energy to manifest and communicate, causing the temperatures to drop in such a dramatic manner. I sensed that I was being watched.

I turned slowly in the direction of the tree line and caught a glimpse of what appeared to be a person crouching down at the water's edge. I took a step or two closer and allowed my eyes to adjust in the dark. There he was; a man in uniform, canteen in hand. The soldier looked up at me, turned and disappeared. I stayed glued in that same spot, hoping he would reappear. After an hour without any further activity, I left for home.

Since that night, I have ventured to the creek bed many times both for my own personal investigations and while conducting walking tours. I love watching the reactions my guests have while at this very special location. Not all of the visitors experience the same type of phenomena as one another. Each of us has our very own gift that enables us to hear, see or even smell at a greater degree than others may be able to.

On one occasion, I had a number of retired police officers from a large metropolitan area on my tour. While at the creek bed, one of them described what he smelled as the unmistakable stench of fresh death. As a police officer, he was certainly qualified to make such a comparison. Oddly though, he was the only one in his group who was able to experience this scent.

Sometimes a guest on the tour will feel as though they are being pushed, almost like someone or something is shoving past them in a hurried fashion. Perhaps these soldiers at the creek are still in battle to this very day.

I have recorded disembodied voices crying out, "Help us if you can. God help us." Those cries may have been uttered in a last desperate plea for help. Help which sadly never came. As I listened to the recording over and over, I truly wish that someone had been there to help those poor soldiers. I sat in silence, swallowing back the tears that always threatened to rise when I knew there was nothing I could do to help ease the pain of those trapped in this agony forever. Wanting to save them from what happened so many years ago left me feeling as helpless as they did on that fateful day.

Ghostly figure at the Haunted Creek Bed
Photo courtesy of Paulette Kozemko

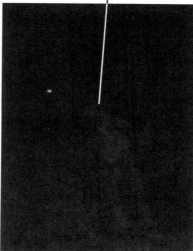

Closeup of figure at Creek Bed

A Watchful Eye

I was going over evidence from an investigation the previous evening, when I noticed a young girl, maybe nine or ten, hovering back and forth outside of the entrance to the shop. She seemed unsure of whether she should enter the store or not but it didn't take her long to make a decision. The bell hanging from the top of the door jingled cheerfully when the girl casually let the screen swing closed.

I gave her a smile and since she seemed occupied in her own thoughts, I left her to them. She had the look of someone with a story to tell but such stories couldn't be forced out, or even coaxed. She would have to come to me when she was ready.

She studied the pictures of our paranormal investigators on display, reading each name and title. Her lips silently mouthed each word, committing them to memory and when she lingered over my picture, I joined her along the wall.

"I'm Spooky," I introduced. "Can I help you with something?"

"I'm Avery," she replied. There was a hesitation before continuing. "Do you think that ghosts can be nice?"

"Absolutely," I waited and when she didn't respond, I spoke again. "Have you had an encounter with one?"

Avery shook her head, then stopped and shrugged helplessly. "Maybe. I don't know…"

Avery's family had just recently moved to Gettysburg, having bought a plot of land southwest of the town. They built a new home there and eagerly moved in just before the start of the school year, so Avery could start fresh. She was a bright thing, with beautiful fair hair. But it was more than her appearance that made her special.

It was after they had moved into their new home that Avery's parents realized that with new work schedules, their little girl would be left on her own for about half an hour each day after school. They fretted and tried to make new arrangements but Avery just gave them her sweet smile and promised that she could manage for such a short period of time. It took weeks of persuasion but eventually her parents agreed.

The first day of school came and Avery happily threw herself into her new classes and meeting new friends. It was such a good day that as the school bus came rounding the corner to her drive, she had almost forgotten that neither of her parents would be home to greet her.

As Avery skipped down the steps, she turned to wave good-bye to her new friends and the bus driver. The bright yellow tail of the bus disappeared in a cloud of dust and she turned to wind her way up to the house, taking her time. She danced this way and then that way across the gravel, kicking at a rock just to see how many times it would bounce before settling in once again.

She laughed and let her gaze settle on the house, going window by window, counting the panes of glass. On the second floor, her game stuttered to a halt when she reached the window that would be the living room.

A woman, dressed entirely in black, stood watching. She was older, bits of gray streaking through her faded brown hair, but still attractive. She leaned against the windowsill, one gloved hand resting on the glass, the other holding back the laced curtain. Avery was uncertain of how she knew, but there was something sad about her, something that had been waiting for too long.

With trembling hands, Avery dug out her house key and sprinted up the porch steps and practically threw open the door in her haste. Instead of being afraid of who this woman was, she instead felt intruded upon and wanted to know why she was in her house. She dumped her backpack in a puddle on the kitchen floor and ran upstairs to find the right window.

She hunted through every room of the second floor, calling out again and again but no one was there. Feeling more confused than ever, Avery returned to the living room window and peered out, both hands resting on the sill. The wood was warm to the touch, not what she would have expected. She thought the room was supposed to feel cold, or dangerous somehow, but it was the same as it had been yesterday, and the day before that.

The view looked out on the front drive, all the way to the bus stop where Avery would hop down every day after school.

"Are you watching over me?" she asked the silent room. There was no reply and Avery was unsure if she felt disappointed or relieved.

She stood in that spot, straining to feel or hear something until she saw her mother's car pull off the road. Avery sighed and returned to the kitchen to pick up her things that had been tossed aside earlier.

"Good day at school?" her mother asked at dinner.

Avery nodded and stabbed at her piece of chicken. She wasn't sure if she should say something to her parents about the mysterious woman, and instinct warned her that it would probably be a bad idea. After all, she had worked so hard to stay by herself and if she said that there was an unknown woman walking around the house, it would probably scare them enough that she wouldn't be allowed to stay by herself ever again.

"Anything interesting happen?" her fathered prodded, smiling lazily as he sipped his coffee.

"No, not really," Avery said as she lowered her gaze. "But I'm sure something interesting will come up soon enough."

* * *

Avery descended the steps, waving good-bye to her friends, the next day. She had been waiting all day for this moment, to see if maybe she had just imagined this woman in black. Walking up the drive, she hummed to herself, keeping her gaze focused on the one particular window.

Nothing. No one there.

Feeling a little annoyed with herself for letting her imagination get away from her the previous day, Avery dug into her pocket for the house key, slowing down to enjoy more time outside. She looked all around, at the late blooming flowers to the leaves that were still bright green. When would they start to change colors, she wondered.

Avery stopped short; however, when she looked up to see the woman in black staring down at her. From such a close distance, she could see the lines weighing down her face. She was still, a silent statue that kept her gaze focused on Avery, who stared back in a similar frozen state.

The woman didn't so much as twitch, even as Avery crept her way up the porch steps and out of sight. She hurriedly opened the door and stopped just inside. Avery closed her eyes and listened but there was nothing out of place, just as it had been yesterday. She knew that if she ran upstairs, there would be no indication that a woman had been standing at the window, no print in the carpet to hint at a bodily weight. Even so, she walked up the stairs to look.

As she had the previous day, Avery stayed in the room until her mother arrived home but this time waited for her to come looking.

"Start your homework yet, Avery?" her mother asked, poking her head into the room.

"What was this place before we built our house here?" Avery replied, ignoring the question of homework.

Her mother stopped and wrinkled her brow in thought. "I'm not entirely sure. I know that there used to be another house here. It was an old ruin. We had to tear it down before we could start plans for our home. Why do you ask?"

Avery shrugged, "I was just curious to know more about it."

"You know those old artifacts your father keeps in his study were found on the property, right?" her mother said, "I don't know how much you heard of some of the problems we had when we started construction here."

Avery shook her head, "I remember there were some problems but you guys didn't talk about it around me that much."

Avery's mother hesitated and then sighed, "Well, apparently there were some… problems." There was further hesitation. "Several of the construction workers claimed they saw Civil War soldiers. They said they would just appear throughout the day and it caused a lot of problems in keeping to the original schedule."

"I never knew that," Avery murmured, "So it was already haunted. Was there ever any mention of a woman in black?"

Her mother watched her daughter closely, "Why do you ask, Ave?"

Avery straightened and shook her head, "Oh, no reason, I was just curious." She gave a false smile and brushed back her blond hair. "I've heard stories about widows who would keep watch

18

for their sons going off to war and all of that. But since it's a new house, I doubt there would be overlap, right?"

"Well, part of our new foundation is based on the old house," her mother replied. "That section was still in good shape and it helped expedite the process. Actually in this wing. From here to the edge of the house." She shrugged. "I don't know if that would mean anything to you or not."

Avery fell silent with a pensive look, rolling the information over in her head.

* * *

Avery chewed over the information she had been given as the weeks went by. The woman never appeared while she was inside the house but Avery imagined that she could feel her presence and would sometimes engage in one-sided conversations about her day or of childhood troubles. It reassured her that the spirit, whoever she was, remained a benevolent one.

Shortly before Thanksgiving, Avery came home, skipping along the gravel and kicking at the piles of raked leaves along the edge of the drive. She had exciting news for her ghostly guardian and was anxious to run up to the living room and talk. It surprised her that her mother's car was hanging out of the carport. Her mother was never home before she was.

Avery's eyes drifted up to the window but there was no serious face with the sad eyes looking down at her. She waited for a moment, almost expecting the woman to brush back the curtain with a grin and mouth "gotcha" down at her. But no such thing happened and Avery knew why. The woman had started watching over her when no one else could be there, but when there was another person, another mother in the home, she was no longer needed.

* * *

"Mom changed her work schedule so she could be home when

I was," Avery explained. "I think she started to get worried when I was asking her about ghosts."

"So the woman hasn't appeared since then?" I asked.

Avery hesitated.

"You still feel her in the house?" I guessed.

She nodded. "And it's not just me anymore," she said quietly. "Now both my Mom and Dad hear footsteps in the middle of the night, going down the hallway but it's not me."

"What do you hear, Avery?"

"The footsteps," she replied.

I waited patiently for her to continue.

"And I know she's watching me. When I walk to the house, when I'm doing my homework, when I'm sleeping. She's always watching over me now... like a guardian angel."

The original house and land it exists on
Photo courtesy of Anonymous

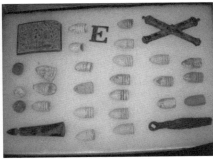

Artifacts found on property
Photo courtesy of Anonymous

The Widow's Cottage

Emily knew the very moment he declared he was going off to war that she would follow. The young couple had only been married for eight short months. It had been a difficult start for the pair. Each had suffered the loss of their last surviving parent, leaving them only each other to rely upon in their time of grief. She simply could not bear to have her beloved walk out the door, leaving her behind, as she was certain she would never see him again. Joseph knew better than to argue against it as in the end, he was certain she would prevail. Having never ventured beyond their hometown in Virginia before, they packed their few belongings hastily and set out on the long and arduous road that would eventually lead them north to Gettysburg. Neither was ever to return home again.

It was July 1st by the time Joseph and Emily arrived in Gettysburg. General Mead was newly appointed to command the Union Army. He chose the Leister Farm House as his headquarters, which was a mere 3/8 of a mile from where the Widow's Cottage stands today. Lydia Leister, a widow herself, was quite startled when General John F. Reynolds' troops surrounded her humble two-room farmhouse, which sat between Cemetery Ridge and Taneytown Road. Fearing for her children's safety, she abandoned her home and went to stay with relatives on Baltimore Pike for the remainder of the battle.

Once on the battlefield, Mead was given tragic news – his good friend, General Reynolds, had been killed. He fought back his tears and shouted out new orders to his men. Mourning would just have to wait.

The young bride clutched the precious photo of her husband closer to her bosom as she heard the roar of cannons exploding just north of town. Emily had been up since dawn, keeping herself as busy as possible, mending the remains of her tattered garments from the difficult journey. With each stitch, she wondered how long until he returned. She gazed out from the entrance of her small tent that had been set up the day before, trying to count the other tents in their encampment. She lost track after twenty. Surely the fighting would have to cease soon.

It was right at dusk when she finally finished gathering wood for the fire. She thought back to the warmth and comfort of their modest wood framed house with its single fireplace and she found herself wishing they had never left home. Damn this war.

A cloud of dust rose over the hill. At last, the men were returning to camp. Wiping the tears from her eyes, she anxiously awaited Joseph. She would be strong. He mustn't see her tears. One by one the soldiers returned. Each looked as if they had stared death in the eyes and in all likelihood, they had. Their uniforms were caked with mud, sweat and dried blood. She saw that some were badly injured and winced each time they cried out in agony. Joseph nearly collapsed next to her as she wiped his sunburned brow with a cool, damp cloth. He looked up at her with a still boyish grin and gave his thanks. Little did they know that this would be the last night she would spend in her husband's arms.

The next day, she waited just as she had the day before, but he did not return. She went around to the surviving men of his regiment, begging to be told what had become of her beloved Joseph. They hung their heads and muttered sadly that they just didn't know. That night, she sat alone in her tent, sobbing.

As morning came once more, against the advice of the soldiers, she set out to find her husband. Emily knew that she could not go on without him. The Confederate Army had set up barriers across Baltimore Street while the Union Army had positioned themselves along East Cemetery Hill and Taneytown Road. With no regard to her own safety, the grief-stricken Emily wandered between the lines as sharpshooters took aim at one another. Somehow escaping the flying bullets, she made her way past the enemy lines to Culp's Hill. Perhaps her husband was on that field, waiting for her to find him. But she could go no further.

Emily was shocked to see the carnage before her. Blood was everywhere as was the smell of death. Tears ran down her cheeks as she saw men writhing in pain. Unable to bear looking into their frightened eyes, she purposely avoided their stares as she carefully stepped around the bloodbath, continuing her search for Joseph. Dropping to her knees, Emily's delicate hands beat the ground with all of her desperation and despair. How could this be happening, she wondered. Knowing she had to continue, she looked up, finding a familiar face in the waves of strangers. Staggering to her feet, Emily rushed to the young man who had been a part of Joseph's regiment.

He recognized Emily at once and stretched out his hand to her. She took his hand and knelt next to him. Seeing the stomach wound, she offered him what comfort she could as he took one last pained gasp of air and died in her arms. After taking the time to send up a last prayer, Emily wiped the blood from her trembling hands and tried to forget what she had just witnessed. She could not, however, shut out the thought, the possibility that out there on this blood-soaked field might lay her beloved husband. Her searched continued long into the night with no sign of Joseph.

For the next several weeks, the citizens of Gettysburg noticed a grief-stricken women walking along the streets, a locket dangling from her hand. When approached, she just looked straight ahead with a blank expression on her face. As the town began its massive cleanup in the aftermath of the battle, the townfolk soon forgot all about the grieving widow and she was not seen in human form again.

On the morning of November 19, 1863, President Lincoln rode his horse out to the grounds of the National Cemetery. Following behind him was a precession of townspeople and widows. Over 15,000 attended the dedication ceremony where Lincoln gave his famous Gettysbug Address. A large, black, wrought-iron fence separated the Soldier's National Cemetery from the Evergreen Cemetery. The National Cemetery was established to pay tribute and honor to the dead. Row after row of white stones mark the graves of the Unknown Soldier. Is our widow's husband among them?

Today, there is a small house which sits directly across the street from the National Cemetery along Taneytown Road. The very last sighting of Emily, Joseph's widow, was at this location. Many have reported hearing the torturous cries of a woman in agony while in the home. A shadowy figure often appears in video and on still film. It is not unusual for guests to feel a sudden chill as the temperatures drop and they hear the gentle rustle of fabric nearby. There is a single fireplace in this dwelling; similar to the one the young couple had left as they set out on their ill-fated journey. Does she sit by the fire, reminded of far happier days? I believe that the Widow remains here, awaiting the safe return of her beloved – forever bound by their love.

Portrait now hangs in the Widow's Cottage
Photo courtesy of Greg Briggs

Widow Leister Farm
Courtesy of the Adams County Historical Society, Gettysburg PA

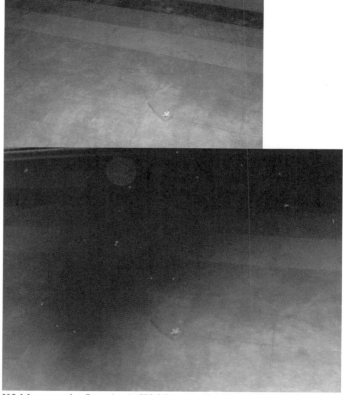

K2 Meter on the floor (top); K2 Meter on the floor immediately after
first shot with captured Shadow not belonging to any guest (bottom)
Photos courtesy of Paulette Kozemko

Sach's Bridge

One of only two covered bridges in Adam's County, Pennsylvania, Sach's Bridge is a destination hotspot for history buffs as well as paranormal enthusiasts. It is nestled off the beaten path, along the winding country roads with battlefields on either side. One really can't help but feel as if they have traveled back in time. Driving along, they are certain that something special awaits them just around the bend. And they are right. As they turn down the dirt covered, dead end road, the bridge looms in the distance.

Being a paranormal investigator myself, I have made many trips out to Sach's Bridge as it has never disappointed. No two trips are ever the same. Each time there is a distinctly different energy to it. Some visits to Sach's are quite peaceful, while other times there is an energy so dark and foreboding that I have to literally force myself to step outside of my vehicle. On those occasions, walking across the bridge is like walking through quicksand. There is sadness present that is undeniable. This beautiful bridge has seen such suffering over the years. I, like many visitors, have reported the feeling of being watched. And it's no wonder, with what has taken place there.

Sach's bridge, once called Sauck's Bridge is 100 feet long.
Built in 1854 by David Stoner, the cost of constructing the bridge
was $1,544.00, or over $30,000 by our standards. On July 1, 1863,
two Union Brigades crossed over Marsh Creek on their way to
Gettysburg. Several days later, Confederate Commander, Robert E.
Lee would divide his troops in half. After suffering a major defeat
in Gettysburg, he sent half of his army across the bridge in retreat,
heading southwest. The remaining half retreated northeast through
Cashtown. In 1968, the bridge was closed to traffic other than
pedestrian in an attempt to preserve the impressive structure. In
June of 1996, however, a flood violently knocked it off its
foundation and sent it up stream. Money was raised and rebuilding
began. At last, the labor of love was complete. Over ninety percent
of the original building materials were salvaged for the cause.

The bridge now sits three feet higher than it had originally.
That very fact may explain why so many visitors capture photos
showing only the upper half of soldiers' torsos. Could these men
be traveling the same path they had in 1863? Sadness filled the air
as the tired men of Lee's army crossed the bridge in the aftermath
of the bloody battle of Gettysburg. Their heads hung low, stomachs
churning; they set up a crude hospital to tend the injured.
Confederate graves were dug. Those too badly injured to travel
were left behind. Tears were shed and promises made. Little did
those men know that in leaving their brothers-in-arms behind as
they made the long journey home that some would remain, forever
searching for a way to escape their fate. Although I myself have yet
to see a full-bodied apparition on my many treks out to the bridge,
a number of other visitors have.

I remember late one evening at Sach's while standing by the
wheel chair ramp, I felt a push on my back. I turned around
quickly, fully expecting to see a person behind me, but there was
no one in sight. I have heard horses neighing and clip clopping
across the wooden planks, the clanging of metal, strange whispers
and gunshots echoing through the woods. But the most amazing
phenomena I have personally experienced would be my encounters

with Caroline.

Caroline is a popular local legend in Gettysburg. The young girl is said to have fallen off of the bridge and tragically drowned many years ago. Unless I have some sort of proof, I tend not to put too much stock in such stories. In fact, I never gave it much thought at all. That is, until Caroline started communicating with me. At first, it was unclear who she was. I would feel a gentle tug at my hand while crossing the bridge, as if a small child was trying to grasp at me. Being a parent myself, I know just how it feels to have a little hand take yours. You are their protector as they cross a busy street, their guide along a crowded sidewalk, a hero they can look up to. I have long been an advocate for children and here at a most unlikely place, a child was crying out. For what, at first, I did not know. Caroline was often times playful and occasionally shy. I called her by name and she responded. I possess several recordings from my communications with her, such as "Where's Daddy?" "Are you a friend?" and "Spooky."

It was on this one particular evening as I walked just beyond the wooden structure that I stopped dead in my tracks. I felt that I was being drawn back to the bridge itself, although I could not tell you for what reason. It was a quiet night, no other people wandering around as there are on a number of other evenings. Over the years, I have learned to trust my feelings. If I am drawn back to the bridge then I listen to that instinct and wait for the result. On that quiet night, I sat down, making myself comfortable on the wooden beams at the base of the bridge. I felt as though I had company.

It was Caroline. I had brought a ball with me, as usual, hoping to entice her out of hiding. I could hear her childlike laughter each time I rolled the ball across the worn planks of wood. I myself was delighted when Caroline honored me by pushing the ball back to me. It wasn't until I had gotten home and began reviewing my voice recordings that I heard her whisper my name, "Spooky." Although I was in the comfort of my own home at the time, it sent shivers down my spine. She had said my name. In all the years I have been in the field of paranormal investigation, this was the first time a spirit had addressed me by name. It was as if she had grown attached to me.

She is afraid of the dark. And so dreadfully lonely, desperately seeking playmates. You mustn't turn your back on Caroline, not ever. In her innocent attempt to find a friend, she has pushed some unsuspecting visitors into the dark waters below. If you bring a ball with you, she might play catch. The question is... do you dare to play catch with her? One family actually fled the bridge in terror, only to jump out of their car screaming after driving only a mile down the road. Why? They all saw the words "Help Me" written on their car window.

It was written from the inside.

Sach's Bridge
Photo courtesy of Johlene "Spooky" Riley

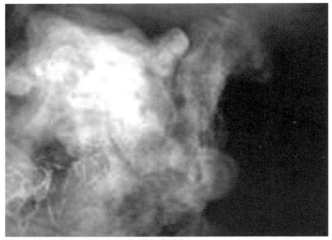

Horse and rider ghost on Sach's Bridge
Photo courtesy of Terry Deitrich

Confederate Soldier in Corn Field at Sach's Bridge
Photo courtesy of Jason "Tater" Yorn

The Dobbin House

Reverend Alexander Dobbin was born in Ireland in the year 1742. He and his wife Isabella Gamble set sail for America in 1773. The Reverend came to the New World as a missionary for the Reformed Presbyterian of Ireland. One year later, he purchased a three hundred acre tract of land and began construction on what would soon be the couple's new home.

In addition to being a home for the Irish-born couple and their ten children, the massive structure played host to a number of other things. It was a classical academy of music, which was the first of its kind on this side of the Potomac, a theological seminary, and, for a short period of time, a church.

Life in the new land was good to the Dobbin family until tragically, Isabella fell ill and passed away at an early age. After some time of grieving, Mr. Dobbin met and remarried the widow, Mary Angus, who also had nine children of her own.

Many years later, this home became a stop on the Underground Railroad in Gettysburg. If you would dare wander up the original wood steps, you would find the hidden walls of the Underground Railroad, which helped many slaves, reach freedom. This exhibit is open to the public today. Visitors to the exhibit have reported hearing a whisper in their ear, footsteps on the very step they are standing on at that moment and scratching sounds on the wall right next to them.

In 1973, the Dobbin House was placed on the National Registry of Historic Places. It is one of just a few eighteenth century buildings still remaining in Gettysburg.

In 1863, like many buildings in Gettysburg, it was used as a makeshift hospital. Both Union and Confederate soldiers received care here. Well over 50,000 men became casualties in the three-day battle which was fought primarily during daylight hours. Sadly, what might be considered a minor injury today would then often times result in a loss of limb. As was the case of the unfortunate gentleman who broke his thumb. After a slight infection set in, the doctor found he had to amputate the patient's arm up to the elbow.

Given these circumstances, can you imagine how many severed arms, legs and rotting torsos there were in these buildings? Now they couldn't very well leave them indoors; the stench alone would not permit it. They would often times toss them out windows, piling them for a later burial of sorts. Some of these piles were as tall as the second story windows. On occasion, a badly wounded soldier thought dead would even be buried alive beneath the partial corpses.

Visitors take pictures of the Dobbin House, hoping to capture its historic beauty and often times get more than they bargained for. Every once in a while the house disappears in photos, appearing as a black void where the house is meant to be. Although the house has vanished, the flagpole out front remains visible in the photo as well as all the fencing and shrubbery in front, on the sides and behind the house. Not possible unless you are in the Ghost Mecca of the World... Gettysburg.

It was November 2008 when I, and a handful of friends, were

in front of the Dobbin House, taking pictures of the stately building. It was on the chilly side as the sun had set hours ago. There we were, bundled in our winter coats in search of ghosts. Suddenly, a scream broke the silent, frost-filled air. My friend was almost in tears as she handed me back the camera I had loaned her just moments before.

"What's wrong?" I asked.

"What is this? Is this a little girl? She looks so scared and sad," she answered.

I took the camera from her trembling hands and confirmed that it was in fact the image of a little girl. I agreed with my friend, this little one indeed had the look of fear frozen on her face. It was an image not easily shaken from my mind's eye, that's for certain.

The Dobbin House is a popular restaurant now; however, its doors had been closed for hours and the building stood vacant, shutting out the possibility that the image captured was a patron. It was too defined to be considered a reflection on the rippled glass of the window. This was the real deal.

Naturally, we were all anxious to take the picture back home and get a closer look. Tossing off our winter layers, we set up in front of the computer screen to review the picture. Looking closely, we were amazed to see another figure just behind the young girl. An older woman looked down over the little girl's shoulder with a scowl on her face that was downright ominous.

A film crew from a major television network had been in Gettysburg the October of that same year. They were setting up for their broadcast in front of the Dobbin House and reported seeing that same little girl we had captured on still film. Reportedly, they all saw her running from one window to the next, looking out each one. They said they would never forget the fear they saw on that child's face. The house was empty at the time – empty of human beings that is.

The mystery of the little girl and older woman has not yet been solved. I wonder why the girl looks out that window with such a look on her face, or why the woman appears so very stern. The two are bound together from a common experience and I continue to search for their names to complete the story.

Just behind the house is an absolutely charming little courtyard. I offer the guests on my tours a seat on the wood benches. One bench is quite unique. I call it the "hot seat". Why? An eight-year-old Boy Scout sat on that seat while on my tour. He immediately jumped up, shouting that it was too hot. At the time, there would have been no logical explanation for the seat being too hot to sit on as it was December. December in Gettysburg is anything but hot. Naturally, guests start to take pictures of him and that "hot seat". In several of the pictures, there appeared to be a fire glowing around the boy and smoke lifting from his shoulders. Best yet, he smelled of a campfire for the remainder of my tour. This was the first but not last time this was to occur to my guests who dared to rest in the "hot seat". Perhaps this is a residual haunting of a campfire set years ago. Could it be an imprint in time?

Some people have caught pictures of Confederate soldiers sitting on benches that, to the naked eye, appear unoccupied. If guests choose these benches, they are gently pushed aside, a reminder that the seat has already been taken.

Thousands of visitors flock to Gettysburg each year. Some come for the history and some come hoping to see a real ghost. I will never forget one particular tour I gave in the spring of 2009. I was leading the late tour at 11:00pm. I had a total of fourteen guests with me that night. I had escorted my group behind the Dobbin House where the courtyard sits. It was a very quiet night in Gettysburg – no cars passing us in the alleys and literally not a soul roamed the streets.

A young lady on the tour stood at the far end of the courtyard, camera in hand, positioned to take a picture of a reenactor dressed in civilian clothes from the Civil War era. Her first and second attempts were met with disappointing results. Her subject was blurry and out of focus. That could be dismissed as operational error. Her third and final attempt, however, yielded a giant white orb in place of the gentleman she was trying to capture with her camera. Although she could see this man clearly, she was just unable to capture the form that she saw with the naked eye.

The poor woman was quite frantic about this phenomenon and immediately showed her husband the picture, trying to explain the unexplainable. The remaining twelve guests and myself turned our attention to the man in tattered clothing who, at this point, headed in our direction from the Dobbin House parking lot.

He disappeared right before our eyes.

If I had been there all by myself, I would have thought of a way to rationalize and debunk this vanishing act. I would have thought that I must have looked away ever so briefly and perhaps he slipped behind a tree or building. Fortunately, I was not alone and all of us saw the exact same thing at the exact same time. He truly disappeared. With so many eyewitnesses, it would be hard not to believe.

Yes, many visitors arrive in Gettysburg hoping to see a real ghost. Well, those folks on that tour got to see one, no doubt about it. So be careful what you wish for … you might just get it!

Girl's face in Dobbin House Window
Photo courtesy of Tisha Wolf

Dobbin House
Courtesy of the Adams County Historical Society, Gettysburg, PA

American Civil War Wax Museum

I remember first watching the Vincent Price movie "House of Wax" late at night with my younger brother. Our small black and white TV flickered in the corner as our only illumination in the dark room. Oh, how we shivered when the figures came to life before our eyes. With thoughts of the movie still fresh in my mind, I found it too difficult to close my eyes. My collection of Valentine dolls sitting on the shelf facing my bed suddenly caught my attention. I wondered if they, like the wax figures in the movie, would come to life the moment I closed my eyes. I shuddered at the thought and pulled the blanket over my head in complete terror. Eventually nodding off to sleep, I would drift into a dreamscape. I found myself locked in a museum overnight, somehow overlooked by the security guard on duty. It would always seem like a great adventure at first but then turn into a frightening ordeal. I would always wake up just in the nick of time, narrowly escaping imminent danger at the hands of those wax figurines.

The American Civil War Wax Museum has become a Gettysburg landmark since opening its doors on Thursday, April

19,1962. The original owner and operator was C.M. Uberman. Located at 297 Steinwehr Avenue, the attraction contains more than 35 scenes and over 300 life-size figures. This museum has given more than eight million visitors a better understanding of the cause and effect of the Civil War. Many famous guests have graced its threshold over the years. Among them are Mamie Eisenhower, Former Speaker of the House, Newt Gingrich, Kyle Perry, John Schreider and Jeff Shaara.

In the year 2000, the Veterans Park was created on the front lawn of the museum. It is a place of peace and tranquility for many as they rest comfortably on the wood benches. The Great Peace Jubilee marker, which has been proudly stationed in the front exterior of the museum depicts the 50th anniversary of the battle of Gettysburg. It was created in celebration of the first joint reunion of the surviving Union and Confederate veterans. This reunion took place July 1st through July 4th, 1913. In attendance were 53,407 veterans made up of 44,713 Union soldiers and 8,694 Confederate soldiers. Encampment consisted of over 6,600 tents spanning across 280 acres. Every year, from April until November, Living History Encampments are held on this ground. Here, Civil War era reenactors set up camp and allow visitors a fascinating glimpse into the life of the soldier during the war here in Gettysburg, 1863.

Recently, I had the opportunity to live out a childhood fascination with these museums. I was to be locked in after hours. After approaching the proper authorities, we were graciously granted access to this amazing site to conduct a paranormal investigation. Like all the locations we have investigated, we gathered as much information as possible before we began. This, of course, would include interviewing the staff. Some shared more than others. A few said they themselves had their own unexplained phenomena from working for the wax museum. Pens moved mysteriously, doors slamming on their own, whispers heard and movement spotted near the displays. Some employees stated that they hadn't had any paranormal experiences at all while in the building. One particularly cheerful young woman behind the front counter laughed as she said, "I hope you don't find any ghosts. I have to be in here all by myself at night, sometimes." We laughed along with her and gave her a few words of comfort. I explained that even if we were to discover it was haunted that she would be in no real danger. We then gathered up our equipment bags and set forth on yet another ghost hunting expedition. No two investigations are alike and I have come to expect the unexpected.

The museum was now closed to the public. Lights and exhibits had been turned off. It was silent and eerie in the pitch-black building. I glanced back over my shoulder at my team members before gently pushing open the swinging wood door to the museum itself. The eerie feeling increased for all of us at the sight of all of the wax figures staring at us with blank expressions on their faces. The interior was much larger than I had expected. Pleased that we would have so much ground to cover, I powered up the equipment I had brought with me. I knew it was just my imagination, but did that wax figurine of Abraham Lincoln just move his eyes?

Using my EMF detector, voice recorder and infrared video camera, I set up for a session with my partner. I chose the second hallway as a starting point as I felt a strong presence there. At first, all was quiet and uneventful. After about fifteen minutes or so, the activity levels started rising. My partner and I were receiving K2 hits as well as picking up muffled voices on our voice recorders. Best yet, the entity we had encountered seemed to be communicating with us directly. It was an intelligent spirit, not a residual one who was no more than an imprint on time.

On our voice recorders, we heard a man's voice asking, "Ready?"

Ready for what, or who, I wondered.

I placed the K2 on the carpeted floor and asked if the gentleman who had asked if we were "ready" could step closer to the green light and perhaps try to touch it. To our amazement, the lights immediately went up to red, indicating this man had certainly obliged our request. Not more than thirty seconds later, the meter slid a few inches, as if being pushed or kicked. Then there was nothing.

Communication with this spirit had ended, at least for now. I have learned over the years that you can't force them to talk if they don't have an inclination to do so. I moved next to the large theater area. Before me was a rather large and impressive scene straight out of the Civil War. Looking at all of the wax figures below, in various stages of battle, I could almost feel the pain that was frozen on their faces. Just on the far end of the exhibit area, I saw my fellow teammates having some success as well.

They called me over, as it appeared they had found something. Both investigators had first noticed a shadowy figure in the battle scene. They both agreed that it had moved from left to right. Taking a picture right away, they captured a bright ball of energy in movement and then the batteries died on the camera. Sometimes, on investigations, fresh batteries will drain quickly. The spirits on location will use up whatever energy source they can in order to manifest and communicate. We didn't mind at all.

By the end of the evening, we successfully captured over eighteen EVPs – Electronic Voice Phenomena – and an image that was rather remarkable.

At the completion of our intial investigation, all team members agreed that the museum was indeed haunted. We packed up our equipment bags and prepared to leave for the evening. As we walked through the darkened hallways, we once again felt as if we were being watched.

Once outside, our team gathered in front of the building to pose for a quick picture as we always do before leaving. The next morning, I was reviewing the pictures when the last picture caught my eye. It was of the group shot taken just before going home. The face of a man stared through the window directly behind my left shoulder. Perhaps we were right. Someone had been watching us after all. The only question is, was he happy we finally left or was he already missing our company?

Devil's Den

The name Devil's Den just seems to reach out and grab most people. The massive boulders jut up from the earth, making the perfect cover for the Confederate soldiers who fought there on the second day of battle, July 2, 1863. The Rebels clearly had the advantage, hiding behind and between the large rocks as they picked off the Northerners when they would try to advance. Eventually, the Union soldiers turned to mirrors and field glasses to locate the sharpshooters hidden in the den of boulders and were able to fire successfully on them. Once shot, many of these sharpshooters suffered a slow and painful death. Their hiding place was so well chosen that after they had been shot, they slid to the ground inside the narrow crevices where their own men couldn't find them in time.

Devil's Den attracts thousands of visitors each year, many of whom have had eerie experiences while there. A group of my friends were in Gettysburg on a day trip and had asked me to show them around. I readily agreed, of course. After deciding which of us would go in which car, we slowly made our way around the winding roads that lead to the Den. As we gathered outside the cars with our cameras in hand, I explained what had happened during the battle at this location. From the expression on several of their faces, I could tell they were pondering the fate of those poor men so far from home.

There were quite a lot of people there that day, some climbing on the rocks that seemed to reach the sky, others taking pictures facing the tree line. My little group noticed an enormous rock formation that didn't have anyone near it, so we headed off in that direction. While everyone else took off on their own, I sat on one of the boulders. I wanted to take in the scenery and relax a little after the hike we had taken.

In all the times that I had been out to Devil's Den, I had never experienced anything paranormal at all, despite the activity others have reported there. I silently reminded myself that I was really there that day so my friends could enjoy this historic, and yes, haunted location, and not to ghost hunt. I glanced over at my friends who had gathered on top of one of the larger boulders and smiled. They waved me over. When I got to the bottom of the giant rock, I looked up and asked if they were having a good time. They nodded their heads, yes.

One of them pointed out to a distant field and asked if I could see what they were seeing. I looked and did see something but wasn't quite sure what it was. I suggested that we move closer for a better look. Keeping my eyes glued to that same spot the entire time, we made our way over. As we drew nearer, I could make out a figure sitting on a rock. The distance from where we began to the field was much further than any of us had expected.

The man sitting on the rock greeted us. We introduced ourselves and made small talk, learning that he was a reenactor visiting from Georgia. This was his first trip to Gettysburg and he said he was enjoying the visit so far. He said that he had been sitting there for hours, waiting to see if the fellow would come out of the woods again. I asked him about this fellow and he described him as fatigued and wearing tattered clothing. He told us that the man wouldn't talk to him when he saw him earlier that he just walked right past him as if he wasn't even there.

I looked toward my friends. I knew exactly what they were thinking.

"Do you believe in ghosts?" I asked the reenactor.

"I'm not really sure," he replied. "I've never seen one, unless maybe that guy I saw earlier is one. That would be a heck of a story to tell back at camp tonight."

"It sure would," I agreed.

We stood with him for a few more minutes and then wished him luck as we began our walk back to our vehicles. I don't know what made me turn around, but I did. I saw our new friend stand up and turn to wave at us. I waved back. As I did, I saw the fellow he had told us about standing just behind him. He was every bit as worn and fatigued as the reenactor had described. He wasn't even wearing any shoes on his feet.

I yelled to the reenactor that the fellow was right behind him. He cupped his hand to his ear to indicate he hadn't heard me and at the same time, my friends turned around and saw exactly what I was seeing. It was the fellow he had been waiting for to come back. I yelled again for him to turn around but then the figure was gone. Finally, a paranormal sighting at one of Gettysburg's most active locations. It had taken years, but it was well worth it. Best yet, my friends all saw it too. We begrudgingly got in our cars and left. My friends were hooked.

Two of my friends said that their camera stopped working while we were at Devil's Den but that it was working fine now. I explained that in 1863, right after the battle, photographers went to Devil's Den to take pictures of the carnage. Some of these photographers moved the lifeless bodies of the soldiers for better angles. Perhaps the spirits remaining at the Den felt disrespected and did not take kindly to photographers, even modern day ones. I have heard of visitors who, while taking pictures, have had their cameras knocked right out of their hands by an unseen force. Many cameras malfunction, pictures are nothing but blackness and batteries drain at Devil's Den.

The most amazing incident involving cameras that I ever heard was shared with me the first time I was visiting the Den. The couple were in their late fifties and told me about the picture they had captured the summer before. They had taken a picture of what appeared to be a soldier holding a rifle and staring right at them. When they took the picture, he was gone. They shuffled through their photos on their digital camera to make sure they had managed to successfully get the soldier ghost. Much to their relief, they had. They showed it off to everyone who would stop to look.

When they returned home, they tried to upload it to their computer and the machine froze up. Baffled, they took the computer in to be fixed and the technician said that he had never seen anything like it before. It was rendered completely useless. The couple was, of course, upset that their computer was damaged beyond repair; however, they still had that amazing picture in their camera. Undeterred, they headed to the nearest photo store to have their prize picture printed. The clerk informed them it would be about an hour wait so they did a little shopping to pass the time. As they returned to the counter to pick up the print, the clerk approached them with an odd expression on her face.

"I'm really sorry," she said, shaking her head. "Everything was fine with your pictures and then all of a sudden we got to the eighth frame and our whole system shut down. We can't get it back online either. I've never seen anything like this before."

I suppose those spirits at Devil's Den really don't like photographers, but who could blame them. So, when you go to the battlefield where the rocks reach up to the sky, hold your cameras tight and watch your step.

Devil's Den - home of a Rebel Sharpshooter by Timothy H. O'Sullivan
Courtesy of Library of Congress

Devil's Den after battle by Alexander Gardner.
Courtesy of Library of Congress

Jennie Wade's Best Kept Secrets

The following is a tale of three friends bound together for all of eternity.

Mary Virginia Wade was born in Gettysburg, PA on May 21, 1843 to parents James and Mary Filby Wade. Ginnie, as she was called by her friends and family, was the second of six children born to the couple. It was in this home that Ginnie was her happiest. There she met her two closest friends – Jack Skelly and Wesley Culp. The three had spent many days laughing, playing, sharing secrets and planning out their lives. Ginnie's father, like his daughter, had fond memories within this house. When Ginnie was twelve, the family moved from their modest home located at 246 Baltimore Street to their new house on Breckenridge Street. It wasn't long after that his life would turn to despair. Ginnie's father was arrested for larceny and sent to the Alms House, an asylum for the poverty-stricken and the mentally insane.

It was a difficult time for the Wade family. Ginnie and her mother both worked as seamstresses to support the household.

Upon hearing rumors Confederates were headed toward Gettysburg, they could not help but wonder what would become of them – especially without an adult male figure in the home. The women's fear became a reality when in the summer of 1863, Lee's army moved north of the Mason-Dixon Line in an attempt to shift the battle away from Southern soil to the North. The Army of the Potomac followed closely behind.

On June 30th, a group of Confederates approached Gettysburg from the West, arriving at Cashtown in search of supplies. They spotted the Union Cavalry in the town. On July 1st, a large group of Rebels approached Gettysburg and the first shots were fired. The battle had begun.

Ginnie, her mother and two younger brothers left their home on Breckenridge to stay with her sister, Georgia McClellan, at 528 Baltimore Street to assist her with her newborn son.

On July 1st, during the first day of the battle, more than 150 bullets hit the McClellan house during the fighting. The Union soldiers retreated to Cemetery Hill. This move placed Ginny and her family in the middle of the deadly crossfire of the two armies. Countless Union soldiers asked the family to leave the house but they refused to go.

Late in the afternoon of July 2nd, Ginnie noticed that the bread supply was in need of replenishing and knew they would be completely out by the next day. She had been generously handing out fresh bread and cool water to the Union soldiers passing by throughout the day. It was hot, she was tired but she helped her mother prepare more bread that evening. The two women left the yeast to rise until the morning of July 3rd. That evening as Ginnie tried to sleep, perhaps she was thinking of her childhood friends, Jack and Wesley.

The three grew up in Gettysburg together and were very close. Each went their separate ways as they reached adulthood, and responsibilities and opportunities set in. One last secret would go to the grave with them, though.

As a teenager, Wesley Culp took a job as a harness maker. When the owner of the business moved his company to Virginia, Culp followed so he could continue his work. He did, however, stay in contact with his friends and family in Gettysburg. When the war began in 1861, Wesley joined the Confederate Army as a member of Company B, 2nd Virginia Infantry. This decision would have him facing off against his own brother and friends from his hometown. He and Ginnie's longtime friend, Jack Skelly, enlisted in the 87th Pennsylvania Infantry in April of 1861.

Yes, as she tossed and turned that hot, July evening, Ginnie would have wondered about her friends. Would she ever see them again? As the morning sun shined brightly through Ginnie's window on July 3rd, she stretched and felt the hard wood floor under her bare feet as she began her day. After dressing, she took the photograph of Jack Skelly that she had placed on the table beside her bed the night before. By 7:00am, the Confederate sharpshooters had already begun firing. Ginnie ignored the shots and slipped on her apron, tucking Jack's photo into the front pocket before she took out the dough she and her mother had been preparing the previous evening. It was about 8:30am when, while Ginnie was kneading the dough for the much needed bread, a Minie ball splintered through the door and penetrated her left shoulder blade, going through her heart and finally coming to rest in her corset as she fell to the floor. She died instantly, becoming the only civilian to be killed in the battle of Gettysburg. No one really knows for certain which side fired the deadly bullet that took poor Ginnie's life that day, however, the vast majority believe it to have come from an unknown Confederate sharpshooter.

That wasn't the only subject of speculation. It was widely rumored that Ginnie was secretly engaged to Jack Skelly. We will never know the truth. Jack was wounded two weeks earlier in the battle of Winchester where he found himself face to face with their mutual friend, Confederate soldier, Wesley Culp. Knowing that he wouldn't survive his injury, Jack asked his boyhood friend to give Ginnie a note he had written for her. Wesley agreed to deliver the note. He was not able to make good on his promise, however. On the very same day that Ginnie was killed by the stray bullet, Culp was killed in Gettysburg, still carrying the note entrusted to him by Jack. Ironically, Culp was shot and killed on his family's farm at Culp's Hill.

Jack Skelly died of his injuries on July 12th, 1863. He left the world without ever knowing the fate of his two best friends, Ginnie and Wesley. Ginnie's body was taken to the basement of the McClellan home and placed on a table until she could be safely taken to their backyard and buried.

Her name was incorrectly reported in the newspaper as "Jennie" instead of Ginnie as she was known by her friends and family. It was from then on that she was referred to as Jennie Wade. In January, her body was relocated to a cemetery next to the German Reform Church on Stratton Street. Her remains were moved to their final resting place in Evergreen Cemetery in November of 1865, near Jack Skelly. A monument in honor of Ginnie was designed by Anna Miller of Gettysburg and erected in 1900. Many visitors flock to Gettysburg to hear the story of Jennie Wade. Some leave not only enlightened by the intriguing story of the three friends but take with them a ghostly experience or photo as well.

I recall one evening after the walking tour I had given, one of my guests smiled as she approached me, camera in hand. I could tell by the way she was grinning from ear to ear that she must have captured something unusual. The young lady explained that while they were standing outside the home Ginnie had grown up in, she had been taking picture after picture as I had instructed the group to do at the start of the tour. She tilted her head down a bit sheepishly as she confessed that she honestly thought that there would be very little chance to capture anything "ghostly." Even though I had told the group that there would be a good chance of getting some great photographic evidence and personal experiences, she still hadn't quite believed it to be possible. That is, she shared, until she looked over the pictures she had taken. She then offered me a look at the images. She had captured a vivid picture of a woman staring out from behind the parted curtain.

There was no one in the building at the time.

That was the last tour for the night. I said my goodbyes to the group and continued along Baltimore Street, past the witness tree near where the battle of Culp's Hill had occurred. The wooden lantern swayed back and forth in my palm as I made my way down the grassy path. It was a clear and silent night. It was so quiet that I could hear the candle's fire snapping and popping. I opened the glass to extinguish the small flame. It went out easily and I lowered the glass once more. Looking up, I found to my surprise a uniformed soldier not more than 30 feet in front of me. I watched as he reached into his shirt and took out what appeared to be a piece of paper. He looked directly at me for just a brief moment, paper in hand, and vanished. I stood frozen in place, staring at the spot I had last seen this strange apparition. I wondered at first if my eyes were perhaps playing tricks on me, but I knew better.

Since then, I have not seen this soldier again. If I do, I already know what I will say to him. "Are you Wesley Culp? Do you have a letter for Ginnie? It's okay, Ginnie is with Jack now. You may be on your way." I truly believe there is a possibility I saw the image of Wesley Culp on that grassy path along Culp's Hill that night.

Culp's Hill is directly behind the very home that Ginnie grew up in. She, as well as her family and two best friends, had a strong connection to this house. Much energy remains in this place to this day. It makes perfect sense that these spirits would linger at this location. A common misconception people make is that all spirits have boundaries and that they are limited forever in just one location, such a a particular room or building. While in some cases this may be true, but it is more likely they would roam from place to place. A good number of visitors to Gettysburg have reported seeing or capturing an image of Ginnie and her father in the home of her sister, Georgia. I feel that the spirits of Ginnie, her father and her two lifetime friends are in and also near the home that they had such a strong connection to. It was in this house that the three friends met and on the field where they spent many days playing together. It was also on that same field where Wesley Culp met his end without being able to make good on his promise to Jack. The letter Jack penned before his own death never found its way to Ginnie. Jack's final letter remains a mystery to this very day. It was never found – whereabouts unknown.

Jennie Wade's Birthhouse on Baltimore St.
Photo courtesy of the Adams County Historical Society

Jennie Wade
Photo courtesy of the Adams County Historical Society

A Kinship

"I am a Civil War reenactor who has portrayed both North and South. I feel honored to have been visited by these spirits and feel great regard for all the brave soldiers who fought here."

-Lonnie, Civil War Reenactor

Many reenactors report seeing or hearing spirits while in Gettysburg. This is not really surprising if you think about it. It's only natural for the ghostly soldiers to be drawn to or disturbed by a reenactor's appearance, The very clothing that reenactors wear can act as a trigger item for these spirits lingering in Gettysburg, as it would be very familiar to them. Residual hauntings are like imprints on time, much like a tape, repeating itself over and over again. Opposite of this is what we call intelligent hauntings, which can and do interact and communicate with people.

Lonnie is a reenactor who shows both respect and honor for those that served in the Civil War. He is also a reenactor that attracts the ghosts. It was September of 2000 when Lonnie and his wife made their first trip to Gettysburg. The hotel where they were lodging was located along the Baltimore Pike. Lonnie had walked into town earlier in the day to take in the sights on his own. It was nearly dark by the time he made his way back, along East Cemetery Hill to the hotel. He was just passing the Evergreen Cemetery when he saw small flames flickering a slight distance ahead of him.

For a brief moment, Lonnie thought to himself how much the flickering lights reminded him of cannon fire. He quickly dismissed the odd lights and continued on his way past a series of cannons set just off the roadside. As he did this, he stopped dead in his tracks as he was shocked to actually see flames bursting forth from their barrels.

Cemetery Hill played an important role in all three days during the Battle of Gettysburg. The curved sector called the "Fishhook Line" by many was a crucial part of the Union Army's defense line. With its rolling hills, it was a good defensive ground against the Confederate Infantry. In addition, it provided cleared fields, which were used as artillery platforms. However, the main reason it was so crucial to the Union Army defensive line was the fact that three major roads – Emmitsburg Road, Taneytown Road and Baltimore Pike – all met there. Therefore, the Union Army was successfully able to block the Confederate advance on Baltimore or Washington, DC.

The Evergreen Cemetery that Lonnie had passed the night he saw the ghostly cannon flames is a civilian burial ground. Built in 1857, the cemetery keeper's wife, Elizabeth Thorn, who was six months pregnant and whose husband was serving in the military, had the daunting responsibility of burying over one hundred soldiers in this very spot. With the help of her elderly parents, they managed to dig those graves in the sweltering hot July sun as the scent of death lingered in the air.

During a later visit to Gettysburg in 2005, Lonnie was back to visit one of his favorite spots, General Hancock's Statue. This imposing equestrian statue overlooks East Cemetery Hill. As he was gazing out over the lush green fields, he noticed a young Union soldier peeking out from behind the statue who was staring directly at him. The young soldier kept gesturing for Lonnie to come forward. He walked over to where the soldier was and stood next to him for a brief moment. The young lad seemed like he was trying to speak but Lonnie had the feeling that this soldier was not a living person, rather a restless spirit that was seeking help.

"I want to surrender," he muttered to Lonnie.

Lonnie did the only thing he knew to do and reassured the boy that he had his permission to go home. To Lonnie's relief, the figure turned to walk away and faded into thin air. Perhaps after all of those long years of torment, the young man finally went home and found peace.

I know Lonnie personally and he is one of those kind-hearted souls that you just never forget. He reenacts to preserve our Nation's history and as he has shared, to honor those who served. I have no doubt that Lonnie has a special kinship with that little spirit on Cemetery Hill. Who better to help him find the peace he so desperately needed than Lonnie?

A view from East Cemetery Hill
Photo courtesy of Hannah Wicklein

No Rest for the Weary

I met Vee and Wendy in the summer of 2009. The two women had arrived in Gettysburg the evening before and stopped to chat with me outside of our ghost tour location. It's not unusual for visitors to share ghost stories and pictures with me so I wasn't surprised at all when Vee and Wendy began sharing their recent experience.

The pair had booked a room for two nights at a local bed and breakfast nearby known for its "spirited" reputation. In fact, it was that very reason that they had chosen this particular lodging establishment in the first place. They were, like many of our visitors to Gettysburg, hoping to have a paranormal encounter. Upon check in, they were told by the staff that there were ghostly children lingering about and suggested leaving out a small toy for the children to play with. It just so happened that Vee and Wendy had a little, green frog keychain with them.

Upon pressing the frog's belly, a loud croaking sound could be heard. The two thought that surely this would serve just fine. As soon as they reached their room, Wendy slipped her keys from the chain and searched for a suitable place to leave the little frog. After pondering this for a moment or so, she decided to leave it on the floor overnight in hopes of attracting a playful spirit. Well, they got more than they bargained for.

The young ladies were rather tired from their long ride earlier in the day. As they prepared to get some much needed sleep, Vee's last words to Wendy were "I hope that something happens!" It wasn't long after they had climbed into bed that they drifted off to sleep.

Several hours later, both Vee and Wendy were startled awake. The frog erupted in a sequence of "croaks" which eerily filled the dark room. Both women sat straight up in bed and looked first at the keychain and then at each other. It was exactly where they had placed it just a few hours ago. Although they saw no signs of anyone or anything in the room, the croaking sound continued on and off throughout the night, as if being played with. They were afraid to close their eyes or get out of bed. Frozen by fear, they remained awake for the remainder of the evening, discussing their options and waiting impatiently for daybreak. They decided that even though they had already paid for a second night at the B&B, they had no intention of staying.

As soon as the sun rose over the town of Gettysburg, the pair quickly gathered their belongings and left the inn. They went out in search of an alternate place to sleep that night. Finally settling on a nearby hotel, the ladies checked in and once again unpacked their bags. Feeling reassured, they spent the rest of the day shopping and enjoying the sights. It was almost dusk when the two arrived at my shop.

After telling me of their experience the night before, I asked if perhaps they would like to go on a candlelit tour I with me. They agreed that they would like to join me but they had a small favor to ask.

"Sure, what can I do for you?" I responded.

Wendy and Vee exchanged glances but it was Wendy who spoke. "We were so frightened about what happened last night with the key chain that we left the inn without returning the key to the front desk. Could you take it back for us, please? We really don't want to go anywhere near that place again."

I accepted the key from Wendy's outstretched hand and noticed that she was trembling.

I gathered up my guests and began my tour. Near the end of the evening, I ask the group, "Is anyone here sleeping in Gettysburg tonight? Raise your hand if you'd like to hear a bedtime story."

Several hands rose and I told a short little story about each location mentioned. No doubt, I gave a fair number of my guests something to think about later as they tried to sleep.

I had no sooner finished the last story when Vee and Wendy rushed up to me and asked if I thought the hotel they were staying at was haunted. Although I could not say for certain, since I had never investigated that location, I did tell them that I had heard a number of reports of paranormal activity there. Their eyes grew wide.

"Did something happen to you there?" I asked.

They explained that when they left the inn that morning and found another place to stay, they had taken the irksome little frog keychain with them and placed it on a side table in their room. While putting away their clothes and toiletries, the frog began croaking once again. The frog had never before spontaneously croaked until they arrived in Gettysburg.

"Why do you suppose it began croaking again at the hotel?" they asked.

As I was expected back at the shop to prepare for my next tour of the evening, I could only offer a few words of comfort and encouragement before we parted ways. I was left wondering if Vee and her friend Wendy dared to spend their last night in Gettysburg.

One thing is for certain, if they had come to town looking for a fright, I would say that they were not disappointed. One can only imagine about that little key chain. Perhaps a small child, grateful for a new toy, had grown attached to it... maybe a little too attached.

For those who rest their heads in Gettysburg tonight, I wish you sweet dreams.

Bonus Investigation: On the hunt with Spooky

Civil War House:
A Haunted Past

There is a house on Baltimore Street in historic Gettysburg that looks like an ordinary home to most people. With the exception of the plaque proudly mounted on the front of the building indicating it as an authentic Civil War era house, one might just walk past without giving it a second glance. This section of Baltimore Street witnessed the horrors of the battle fought here in 1863. Quite a few buildings in very close proximity to it were taken over by Confederate sharpshooters. Union General Alexander Schimmelfennig hid in one of the homes directly across the street to avoid capture by Confederates. This house is anything but ordinary.

It was a crisp fall afternoon in 2009 when I came in to work to find a message waiting for me on my desk. The note was in regards to a phone call that had come in that morning.

"There's no way I would stay in that house. Not after what the tenant told me about it," said the staff member who had taken the message.

I couldn't wait to hear about this place. I dialed the number, waiting anxiously for the receiver to be picked up.

"Hello?" said the voice on the other end.

I introduced myself and could hear a sigh of relief from the man on the line.

"Thank you for calling back so quickly."

He went on to explain the strange things that had been happening in the apartment he and his girlfriend had recently rented on Baltimore Street. After hearing the sincerity in the young man's voice and given what had been going on at this location, I was more than happy to pay him a visit. Perhaps I would be able to be of some assistance. The initial meeting was scheduled for the next day.

I arrived at the couple's apartment early the next day as promised. The house itself was rather large and situated on a street that was known for frequent paranormal activity. It was once a single-family home that had been recently divided up into three separate rental units. As I walked around to the rear of the building, I could see Culp's Hill not far off. The battle fought there was one of the bloodiest of the Civil War.

I entered the building and using the wooden stairs, made my way up to the couple's apartment on the second floor. I knocked on the door and waited for an answer. The hall had an eerie feel to it, as if I were not alone. The door swung open and the man I had spoken with on the phone greeted me with a handshake. I was escorted in and took a seat in the couple's living room. Shawn and his girlfriend, Mandy, joined me. I took notes as I listened to what they had to share.

The first of the many strange occurrences happened within days of moving into their new apartment. They were in the basement, moving items the previous tenants had left behind to have room to store their own belongings. Mandy was moving things about when she discovered a black box on one of the shelves. She shuddered when she opened it up and discovered a very old typewriter, which she described as creepy. She had no idea just how creepy that typewriter really was. Shawn came over and casually pushed the typewriter and its box over on the dusty shelf.

The light bulb above their heads began to flicker. Shawn reached up to tighten the bulb then went up to retrieve a few of their boxes. After what had only been a couple of minutes, they returned to the basement with the boxes. Mandy shrieked when she saw that the typewriter had moved itself right back to its original resting place on the shelf. The light bulb, which had been tightened just moments ago began to flicker once again. The bulb had been unscrewed. But by whom? They screwed the bulb tight and just as they did, the storage room door slammed shut with a loud bang and the basement went completely black... no lights at all!

The couple told me that they fled to what they thought would be the safety of their apartment. Over the next day or so following that incident, they both convinced themselves that everything that had occurred to them in the basement was most likely just their imagination playing tricks on them.

Several days later, Shawn stood in their kitchen when he felt an unseen hand grab a hold of his arm. The next day, he was standing on his back porch enjoying the last bit of sun before it set for the evening when he felt as if he were being watched. Shawn assumed that it was his girlfriend, so he turned toward the screen door behind him but instead saw a shadowy figure standing inside the hallway. He yanked open the door and the figure ran towards him and then up the stairs to his apartment. Shawn ran after the figure but it had vanished.

Shaken by this experience, he went into his apartment and called for Mandy. After he told her what had happened, she insisted they pack up that very second. Shawn couldn't deny that he was also uncomfortable staying.

"No ghost will run me out of my home!" he declared.

Reluctantly, Mandy agreed to stay, at least for the time being.

I asked the couple about the latest incident that had occurred.

Shawn had been in the upstairs hall, right outside their apartment door smoking a cigarette when he looked up and saw a woman peering around the corner at him. She had very long dark hair, which appeared to be dripping wet. Shawn bolted out of the chair and ran toward the woman. The figure disappeared around the corner. He was surprised that he hadn't heard any footsteps running down the stairs when the figure ran away.

Mandy spoke up. "I really think this place is haunted. Even Shawn, who didn't believe in ghosts, is getting scared. I'm afraid. I just can't explain this stuff away anymore. Do you think you can find out what we have here?"

I told them that I would do my best, asking for permission to look up the history on the house and perhaps gain access to the entire building. They agreed, even calling their landlord to request keys to the unoccupied apartments in the building. The owner agreed to allow me in the other apartments to further investigate as long as I was discreet. After all, haunted apartments are hard to rent. I left the couple's apartment at nightfall, hoping that they both would be able to get a good night's rest. I began my historical research the next day.

Investigations such as this are like giant jig saw puzzles and I love trying to put all the pieces together and see the whole picture. I spent the better part of the day at the local historical society searching for information on the house. Although I was easily able to find information about the neighborhood, I couldn't find a single thing pertaining directly to the house itself.

I collected my equipment and several team members of our paranormal group and returned to the house on Baltimore Street to spend the night and collect evidence to either support or deny paranormal activity. The couple had vacated their residence for the duration of our investigation. We started in the third floor apartment. There had been nobody living in this apartment for the last two years and felt that there must be a reason for it. When we were on the second floor, I thought I heard a disembodied voice, although I couldn't be sure. As soon as we turned the key in the door on the top floor, I could feel the energy, as strong as I had ever felt. The air was thick, making it difficult for us to breathe. We went from room to room, acquainting ourselves with the layout before we began the communication session. The former tenants had left behind a few pieces of furniture. The little room at the back of the hall was where I felt the most negativity. While in the room, the door slowly closed. I tried to debunk it by opening the door again and watching to see if shifting of weight on the floor could have caused the door to close due to improper hanging. It remained open; however, without closing again while we stood and watched. We moved on to the front room of the attic apartment and I sat at the small dining table that was set up in the room.

As I set down a flashlight on the table in front of me, I had the feeling that we were not at all welcome in this apartment. Whichever spirit or spirits were lingering did not appreciate our presence.

"If you want us to leave, we will. All you need to do is douse the light that I have placed on this table," I said to the open room.

No sooner had I spoken those words than the light went out. I had to be sure it wasn't off due to a faulty light bulb or dead battery.

I spoke again, "We promised to leave, however we must make sure this is you communicating with us. Can you please turn that light back on for us?"

The light instantly glowed once again and slowly began rolling in one direction, stopped completely and then rolled in the opposite direction before finally flying off the table, crashing into the wall directly behind me. When the flashlight sailed past my head, I was more than a little startled. I wasn't so much concerned that a moving object had almost caused me bodily harm, but more intrigued at the amount of energy behind this amazing display. It was almost as if this spirit was saying to us loud and clear, "I have done what you asked, now just leave."

The team packed up the equipment and we left to investigate the remaining areas of the house. I went to the basement. I left the lights off, using only my flashlight to guide the way. The stairs were narrow and the ceiling low. I looked for the typewriter, the one the couple claimed had moved on its own. It wasn't a large basement, so I easily spotted it sitting on the shelf where the couple had last seen it. There was something odd about it although I couldn't quite put my finger on just what it was.

I had brought a piece of paper with me that I had planned on placing in the typewriter. It was a long shot, but I was really hoping that perhaps a key or two would strike the paper and a message would appear, or at the very least, encourage the spirit to react in some way. I thought that this spirit was somehow attached to this typewriter and that I should start by moving it as Shawn had. After waiting some time without any activity, I turned my attention to the metal chair that was in the middle of the room. Even though it seemed out of place, I sat down. I turned my flashlight off and sat in silence, hoping for something, anything, to happen. I had almost given up when I felt my hair being gently moved as if someone walking past me had brushed up against me as they made their way by.

Without warning, I was shoved completely off the chair. I scrambled to my feet, heart beating faster than I ever thought possible. I began searching for my flashlight that had dropped from my hand during the fall. I spied it on the floor in the far corner, the light now shining so it was fairly easy to find.

I radioed the other team members that were upstairs and advised them that we were done. We packed up our equipment and left the house. Once outside, we all began sharing our experiences from the evening. Apparently, we were dealing with more than one ghost in this house. We would need to set up additional nights to further investigate and execute a plan of action for the frightened couple in the second floor apartment.

By the time I got home, I was too wound up to sleep and figured I could review the data on our voice recorder for any evidence. I had listened for only 15 minutes when I heard the first of seventeen disembodied voices coming from the device. During the interview with Shawn and Mandy, two voices could be overheard laughing and talking but they weren't clear enough to make out exactly what they were saying. The clearest voice phenomena occurred when we were in the basement. Just before I was shoved off the chair, a voice could be heard saying, "Get out of my way."

After three hours, I turned in for the night. I called the couple the next day to let them know what we had found. Mandy answered the phone on the third ring and I could tell she was out of breath.

I asked if she would be able to meet with us later in the day so we could go over what happened during the first investigation of the house.

"We are moving out of here today," she replied.

"Really, did something else happen?" I asked.

"When Shawn and I got home this morning, we heard noise coming from the basement. We both thought that maybe you and your team were still down there investigating so we opened the basement door and yelled down but no one answered. Then the door slammed shut. We both could hear the keys of the typewriter clicking. We ran upstairs to our apartment. I told Shawn I was leaving with or without him and then we both saw a shadowy figure run through the living room! Thank you for coming in yesterday but we both just want to get out of this place."

I'm sure that what happened in that house would be forever etched in the minds of that couple, just as I am sure that I will be going back there to solve the puzzle. It's what I live for, after all.

To be continued...

Moving typewriter found in the Civil War House
Photo courtesy of Johlene "Spooky" Riley

Civil War Plaque from building
Photo courtesy of Hannah Wicklein

Photo Credits

We would like to thank everyone for the use of their photography.

Please contact Gettysburg Ghost Tours if you have any questions about any of the images you see in the book.

Old Number One
Cannon with ectoplasm- Anonymous
Ghost face by Cannon - Johlene "Spooky" Riley

Forever They May Roam
Woods along Doubleday Avenue - Hannah Wicklein
Orb along Doubleday Avenue - Johlene "Spooky" Riley

Help Us If You Can
Green shadow figure - Paulette Kozemko

A Watchful Eye
Relics found on property - Anonymous
House and surrounding property - Anonymous

Widow's Cottage
Widow's picture - Greg Briggs
Leister Farm - Adams County Historical Society, Gettysburg, PA
K2 Meter on Floor - Paulette Kozemko
K2 Meter on Floor with Shadow Figure - Paulette Kozemko

Sach's Bridge
Horse and rider - Terry Deitrich
Soldier in the cornfield - Jason "Tater" Yorn
Sach's Bridge in day - Johlene "Spooky" Riley